GEORGE AND MARTHA ROUND AND ROUND

For My Mother

www.hmhbooks.com

First Green Light Readers edition, 2011

SANDPIPER and the SANDPIPER logo are trademarks of Houghton Mifflin Harcourt Publishing Company.

Green Light Readers and its logo are trademarks of Houghton Mifflin Harcourt Publishing Company, registered in the United States of America and/or other jurisdictions.

The Library of Congress has cataloged the hardcover edition as follows:
Marshall, James, 1942–1992
George and Martha : round and round / written and illustrated by James Marshall.
p. cm.
Three of the stories that were originally published in
George and Martha : round and round, 1988.
Summary: Three stories chronicle the ups and downs of a special friendship between two hippopotamuses.

ISBN: 978-0-618-98505-0 hardcover
ISBN: 978-0-547-51982-1 paperback

[1. Friendship–Fiction. 2. Hippopotamus–Fiction.] I. Title.
PZ7. M35672Gef 2008
[E]–dc22
2007025742

Manufactured in China
LEO 10 9 8 7 6 5 4 3 2 1
4500282833

Ages: 7–8
Grade: 2
Guided Reading Level: L
Reading Recovery Level: 19

GEORGE AND MARTHA ROUND AND ROUND

written and illustrated by

JAMES MARSHALL

Green Light Readers

HOUGHTON MIFFLIN HARCOURT

BOSTON   NEW YORK

THREE STORIES ABOUT THE BEST OF FRIENDS

STORY NUMBER ONE

THE CLOCK

George gave Martha a present
for her birthday.

"It's a cuckoo clock," said George.

"So I see," said Martha.

"It's nice and loud," said George.

"So I hear," said Martha.

"Do you like it?" asked George.

"Oh yes indeed," said Martha.

But to tell the truth,

the cuckoo clock got on Martha's nerves.

The next day

George went to Martha's house.

Martha was not at home.

And the cuckoo clock

was not on the wall.

"Maybe she likes it so much

she took it with her," said George.

Just then he heard a faint

"Cuckoo . . . cuckoo . . . cuckoo."

To George's surprise,

the cuckoo clock was at the bottom

of Martha's laundry basket.

When Martha returned,
she couldn't look George in the eye.
"It must have fallen in by mistake,"
she said. "I do hope it isn't broken."
"Not at all," said George.
"The paint isn't even chipped,
the clock works just dandy,
and the cuckoo hasn't lost
its splendid voice."

"Would you like to borrow it?"
asked Martha.

George was delighted.

He found just the right spot for it, too.

Wasn't that considerate of Martha
to lend me her clock? thought George.

"Cuckoo," said the clock.

STORY NUMBER TWO

THE TRIP

George invited Martha

on an ocean cruise.

"Is *this* the boat?" said Martha.

"Use your imagination," said George.

"I'll try," said Martha.

Very soon it was raining cats and dogs.

"This is unpleasant," said Martha.

"Use your imagination," said George.

"Think of it as a thrilling storm at sea."

"I'll try," said Martha.

"Lunch is served," said George.

And he gave Martha a soggy cracker.

Martha was not impressed.

"Use your imagination," said George.

"Oh looky," said Martha.

"What a pretty shark."

"A shark!" cried George.

George took a spill.

"But where's the shark?" he said.

"Really," said Martha. "You must learn to use your imagination."

STORY NUMBER
THREE

THE ARTIST

George was painting in oils.

"That ocean doesn't look right," said Martha.

"Add some more blue.

And that sand looks all wrong.

Add a bit more yellow."

"Please," said George.

"Artists don't like interference."

But Martha just couldn't help herself.

"Those palm trees look funny," she said.

"That does it!" said George.

"See if you can do better!"

And he went off in a huff.

"My, my," said Martha.

"Some artists are *so* touchy."

And she began to make

a few little improvements.

When George returned
Martha proudly displayed the painting.
George was flabbergasted.
"You've ruined it!" he cried.
"I'm sorry you feel that way," said Martha.
"I like it."
Martha was one of those artists
who aren't a bit touchy.

Word Search

Find: cruise, cuckoo, artist, splendid, dandy

S	D	C	U	C	K	O	O
A	P	A	E	K	X	N	S
R	G	L	R	Q	M	T	M
T	F	K	E	W	S	K	S
I	H	V	L	N	A	D	P
S	L	D	A	N	D	Y	U
T	S	T	H	O	P	I	F
C	R	U	I	S	E	G	D

Fill in the blank. Answers at the bottom of the page.

1. George gave Martha a cuckoo clock for
   her_____.

2. George was delighted when Martha let him
   _____ her clock.

3. George gave Martha a soggy
   _____ for lunch.

4. George was scared of Martha's imaginary
   _____.

5. Martha thinks George's ocean would look
   better with more _____ paint.

6. George thinks Martha _____
   the painting.

More fun activities to do at home!

- Draw a cuckoo clock. What time is it? Does your clock make a "cuckoo" sound every hour, or does it sound like something else?

- Use your imagination! Draw a picture of the boat you would sail on an ocean cruise.

- Draw a picture of you and your best friend on the beach.